hardie grant EGMONT

Swamp Race
published in 2013 by
Hardie Grant Egmont
Ground Floor, Building 1, 658 Church Street
Richmond, Victoria 3121, Australia
www.hardiegrantegmont.com.au

A CiP record for this title is available from the National Library of Australia.

Text, illustration and design copyright © 2013 Hardie Grant Egmont

Illustrations by Craig Phillips
Design by Simon Swingler

Printed in Australia by Griffin Press, an Accredited ISO AS/NZS
14001:2004 Environmental Management System printer.

1 3 5 7 9 10 8 6 4 2

The paper this book is printed on is certified against the
Forest Stewardship Council® Standards. Griffin Press holds
FSC chain of custody certification SGS-COC-005088. FSC
promotes environmentally responsible, socially beneficial
and economically viable management of the world's forests.

FSC
www.fsc.org
MIX
Paper from
responsible sources
FSC® C009448

ZAC POWER

SWAMP RACE
BY H.I. LARRY

ILLUSTRATIONS BY CRAIG PHILLIPS

hardie grant EGMONT

CHAPTER 1

Zac Power pulled another shirt out of the washing basket. He was not having a good night.

Zac's parents had been called into his school for a meeting. The principal had noticed that Zac had missed a lot of school lately, and she wanted to know why.

The truth was that Zac was a highly

trained secret agent for the Government Investigation Bureau (GIB for short). He had to keep skipping class to go on dangerous spy missions.

But the principal wasn't allowed to know that. It was all top secret. As far she knew, Zac was just a normal kid. Zac's parents would have to come up with a good story to explain why he kept disappearing. Zac's parents and his brother Leon were all spies, too.

As if that whole mess at school wasn't bad enough, Zac's mum had left him at home with a massive load of washing to fold. Zac had been slaving away for ages already and he was only halfway through the huge basket of clothes. He reached down again and pulled out a pair of Leon's underpants.

'Ugh!' he groaned. 'Gross!'

The worst bit was that Zac's parents had decided he needed a babysitter while they were out. Usually, Zac would be left with Leon at times like this. But Zac's geeky older brother was out tonight, too.

Which meant that Zac was stuck at home with some random babysitter. And all night she'd done nothing but watch TV and talk on her phone.

It's so unfair! Zac grumbled to himself. *I've been to the MOON and back by myself, but I'm not allowed to stay home alone for a few hours? It doesn't make any sense!*

Zac decided to take a break from folding the washing. He pulled out his SpyPad (the high-powered tablet carried by every GIB agent) and began checking his SpyMail.

A sudden voice behind Zac made him jump. The babysitter was coming down the hall towards him, still talking into her phone.

'Yeah, OK,' she was saying. 'I'll give it to him now.'

Zac quickly stashed his SpyPad into the washing basket, hiding it from view just as the babysitter walked into the room.

'Hi, Zac,' she said.

'What do you want?' said Zac grumpily.

'Don't be so cranky,' said the babysitter, smiling. 'I've got something for you.'

Yeah, right, thought Zac. *What could you possibly have that I'd want?*

But Zac's mouth dropped open as he saw what was in the babysitter's hand. It was a shiny silver disk. A mission from GIB.

Zac stared at the girl. Obviously this was no ordinary babysitter!

The babysitter flashed a GIB card. 'Agent Blizzard at your service,' she said. 'Go on, you'd better read the mission.'

Zac pulled his SpyPad out of the washing basket and stuck the disk inside.

'You'd better get going,' said Agent Blizzard. 'Your brother is waiting across

CLASSIFIED

MISSION INITIATED: 6 P.M.
CURRENT TIME: 8.23 P.M.

GIB has received a message from the enemy agent Professor Voler.

Voler has the blueprints for a high-tech spying device called the X-Beam.

Voler says he is willing to give these blueprints away. He has invited you to a meeting on his jet to discuss this matter.

His offer expires at 6:00pm tomorrow.

YOUR MISSION
Meet with Professor Voler and retrieve the X-Beam blueprints.

END

the road to brief you.'

Zac nodded and ran for the door. *Well, he thought, looks like I'll be missing another day of school tomorrow.*

CHAPTER

Zac raced outside and looked around for Leon. He spotted a big laundry service van parked on the other side of the street.

Zac knew that this was no ordinary van. It was the Mobile Technology Lab, Leon's disguised laboratory on wheels. Zac slid open the van door and climbed in. Inside the MTL, Leon was busy tinkering at a workbench. Tinkering was what Leon did best. He was a GIB technical officer, in charge of developing gadgets and organising missions.

'There you are!' said Leon, turning around. 'Time to get moving. You have to be at the drop-off point by 6.30 a.m.'

Leon pushed a button and the MTL started rumbling along the road. Zac noticed that it was driving on autopilot.

'Where's the drop-off point?' Zac asked, glancing at the time on his SpyPad.

8.30 P.M.

'Professor Voler wants us to leave you at a place out in the bush,' said Leon. 'He'll pick you up from there.'

'Why?'

'You know what Voler's like,' Leon said. 'Everything has to be totally secret. He wants to be sure you're alone before you get on his jet.'

Zac nodded. Professor Voler was a strange old thief who lived in an enormous jet. He spent most of his time flying around stealing rare technology.

Zac had met Voler once before, but the old man had escaped before Zac could arrest him.

'So why is Voler giving away this free technology?' Zac asked. 'It sounds like a trap to me.'

'I know,' said Leon. 'We think so, too.

But it's worth the risk if you can get your hands on those X-Beam blueprints.'

'What is an X-Beam, anyway?' Zac asked.

'It's kind of like an X-ray,' said Leon. 'But instead of looking through skin and bone, it lets you see through solid brick and metal. In theory, that is.'

'What do you mean, *in theory?*' said Zac, raising his eyebrows.

'Well,' said Leon, 'that's what an X-Beam is *supposed* to do, but no-one's ever come up with working blueprints before.'

'Until now,' said Zac.

Leon nodded. 'Which is why we need to make sure Voler's blueprints don't fall into the wrong hands. Imagine what would happen if BIG got hold of them!'

BIG were the most ruthless spies in the business and GIB's greatest enemies. It would be a disaster if BIG could make a working X-Beam!

'So, what's the plan for this mission?' Zac asked, leaning on the workbench and glancing out the front window. The MTL was travelling along the open highway now.

'Well, obviously we're not going to send you out there unprotected,' said Leon, picking up what looked like a metal T-shirt. 'This is Electro-Armour, the latest in GIB personal safety gear. It should shield you from just about anything Voler can throw at you.'

'Excellent,' said Zac, grabbing the armour.

'That panel on the front is electrically charged,' said Leon, pointing at the chest. 'It'll zap anything that touches it.'

Zac pulled off his shirt and carefully slipped on the Electro-Armour. While he did that, Leon turned to his bench and pushed a few buttons.

'So that's the plan?' Zac said, putting his shirt back on over the top. 'I just head out to the bush wearing a metal T-shirt, figure out how to get hold of the blueprints and – *whoa!*'

Zac was nearly thrown off his feet. For a moment he thought he had electrocuted himself with the Electro-Armour. But then he realised that the MTL had suddenly started hurtling forward, tearing down the highway at incredible speeds.

'Leon!' Zac shouted, steadying himself. 'What's going on?'

'I've added a few upgrades to the MTL,' said Leon. 'Ready for take-off?'

Zac stared at Leon. 'Ready for *what?*'

Leon just grinned at him.

Zac grabbed hold of the workbench at the front of the truck and stared out the window. Huge flat wings were unfolding from underneath the MTL.

A second later, the van lifted off the ground and soared up into the dark night sky.

'Well?' said Leon, smirking. 'What do you think?'

'It's awesome,' said Zac. 'But if you do something like that again without warning me, I'm going to switch on my Electro-Armour and give you a big hug.'

CHAPTER 3

'How much further?' Zac asked, yawning. He stretched and sat up in his seat.

The Mobile Technology Lab had been flying all night, and Zac could just see the sun starting to rise in the distance.

'Almost there,' said Leon. 'We're coming up to the drop-off point now.'

A few minutes later, Leon landed the

MTL at the edge of some bushland. 'See that big rock over there?' he said, pointing. 'That's where you're supposed to wait. You'd better hurry, too. It's almost time.'

Zac nodded and climbed out of the van. As he watched, the MTL rumbled across the grass and took off into the air again.

Zac walked through the bush and stopped at the rock where Leon had told him to wait. He checked the time.

6.31 A.M.

Voler had said to be here at 6.30 a.m. but so far Zac couldn't see any sign of –

CRASH!

Zac's eyes darted upwards. Something big and heavy was crashing down through the trees above his head. Zac leapt out of the way just in time.

THUD!

A big wooden crate hit the ground — right where Zac had been standing!

Zac walked over and looked at the crate. Then he stared up at the sky. Zac knew Professor Voler's jet was protected by advanced cloaking technology. It was obviously hovering somewhere above him, but Zac couldn't see it.

Am I supposed to open the crate? wondered Zac. *It's been nailed shut!*

CRASH!

Something else was coming down through the trees.

Zac took cover again.

CLANK!

A big metal crowbar landed neatly on top of the crate.

Right, thought Zac. He jammed the crowbar into the crate and levered off the lid. Inside was what looked like a heavy black wetsuit.

Sitting on top of the suit was a handwritten note.

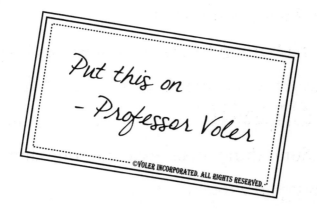

Put this on
— Professor Voler

©VOLER INCORPORATED. ALL RIGHTS RESERVED.

Zac pulled the suit on over his clothes. A metal rectangle, the size of a shoebox, bulged out the back of the suit.

On the sleeve of the suit, Zac noticed a tiny control stick and a row of buttons. He tapped at the controls but nothing happened.

Maybe the suit got damaged in the fall, he thought. But then the box on Zac's back started jolting wildly. He staggered forward. *What on earth —?*

Three long metal blades were unfolding out of the box. The blades flattened above Zac's head, and then started spinning around and around like the ones on a helicopter.

'Whoa!'

Suddenly, Zac lifted off the ground. The helicopter blades sent leaves flying as he rose up between the trees.

Zac jiggled the control stick but it was no good. Someone was steering his Chopper Suit and it wasn't him.

Voler must have this thing hooked up to a remote control, thought Zac.

The Chopper Suit flew up through the air, guided by its invisible pilot. Zac was jolted across to the left, then straight up, then to the right again. Then he stopped, hovering on the spot.

Zac peered around for some sign of Voler's cloaked jet. He could hear the rumbling of a big engine, but he couldn't see anything.

HISSSS-CLUNK!

A hatch suddenly opened up in the empty sky above Zac.

A-ha! Zac thought. *This must be it.*

As the metal door hissed open, the jet's cloak flickered slightly. Zac caught a glimpse of the huge flying machine floating above him.

The Chopper Suit started moving again and Zac was lifted up through the hatch, into the jet.

HISSSS-CLUNK!

The hatch hissed shut beneath Zac's feet. With one final jolt of the Chopper

Suit, he touched down inside the jet.

There was a big round button on the chest of Zac's suit marked 'REMOVE'. Zac pushed it.

SNAP!

The Chopper Suit popped right off his body and landed in a heap on the floor.

Zac looked around him. He was in a big round room filled with jet-packs, parachutes, and other kinds of personal flying machines.

There was a ladder leading up out of the room. Zac climbed up and found himself inside a narrow hallway.

Zac walked down and opened the door at the end. He stepped into an enormous lounge room. It was filled with beautiful antique furniture and decorated with priceless paintings and statues. All around the walls were shelves stuffed with hundreds of stolen artefacts and gadgets.

'Ah,' said a voice. 'Zachary! You're just in time for breakfast.'

Zac turned and saw Professor Voler sitting at his ornate wooden tea table, dressed in his usual suit and tie. He was buttering some toast and smiling warmly at Zac.

Then Zac saw something that made his stomach turn. Voler wasn't alone.

Sitting in a chair opposite the professor was BIG agent Caz Rewop.

CHAPTER 4

'Caz!' Zac snarled.

12-year-old Caz Rewop was one of BIG's most dangerous spies. Zac had met her several times before. He knew she was nothing but trouble.

Caz didn't look too happy to see Zac either. 'Agent Rock Star,' she growled, leaping to her feet.

She was carrying a big stick with a BIG logo stamped onto the handle. Caz gave it a flick, and a bright red cord of electricity shot out the end. She held the gadget like a whip towards Zac, ready to strike.

Zac looked from Caz to Voler and back again. *WHAT is going on?*

'What's *he* doing here?' Caz demanded, glaring at Voler.

'Me?' said Zac. 'Why are *you* here?'

'Everyone, please, settle down,' said Voler, standing up calmly. 'If you'll kindly take your seats, I will explain everything.'

Zac and Caz didn't move. They just stood there, frozen on the spot, glaring at each other.

'Come now,' smiled Voler. 'Your break-fast is getting cold.'

He pulled the cover off a tray piled high with bacon, eggs, sausages and hash browns.

Zac sat down at the table, shaking his head.

He knew Voler was nothing but a thief and a liar, and he didn't trust the old man's kindness for a second. But co-operating with Voler seemed like his best chance of getting the X-Beam blueprints.

Caz seemed to agree. She gave Zac one last glare, then switched off her Electro-magnetic Whip and took her seat again.

'There we are,' said Voler cheerfully,

beginning to serve out the breakfast. 'Now, I suppose you're both wondering about those X-Beam blueprints.'

'What do the blueprints have to do with *him?*' said Caz angrily, stabbing a finger in Zac's direction. 'You said you were going to give them to BIG!'

'What?' said Zac, his eyes darting over to Professor Voler. 'You said you were giving them to GIB!'

'Actually,' Voler corrected, 'what I *said* was that I am willing to give the blueprints away. I never said to *whom.*'

Voler put a plate of food down in front of each of them. Then he reached into his pocket and pulled out a small plastic toad.

'Inside this plastic toad is a Data Storage Device, or a DSD, which contains everything you need to build a working X-Beam,' Voler explained.

'And how do we get it?' Zac asked.

'I propose a competition,' said Voler, picking up a silver knife and fork. 'In a few hours, the two of you will be dropped off in the Murky Swamp. This DSD will be hiding somewhere down there. Whoever finds it first may keep it.'

'That's it?' said Caz suspiciously.

Voler nodded. 'That's it.'

'But why?' asked Zac. 'Why are you doing this? You've spent your whole life stealing things from other people! Why are you suddenly giving stuff away?'

'Those blueprints mean nothing to me,' said Voler with a wave of his hand. 'Look around you. I have all the riches I need. What I want now is to be *entertained*.'

'Entertained?' said Zac. 'You mean this whole thing is just some twisted game for your amusement?'

'Yes and no,' said Voler. 'I shall certainly enjoy watching you compete. But I assure you this is far more than just a game.'

He took a sip from his tea cup and then continued.

'There are dangerous things in that swamp, Zachary. Toxic waters. Creatures that are big enough to swallow you whole.

Not to mention a few of my own little surprises.'

'And what if I refuse?' demanded Caz. 'What if I don't want to play your game?'

'Then Zachary gets the DSD all to himself,' said Voler. 'Of course, if it is Zachary who refuses, the DSD is yours.'

Zac stared at Voler. There was no way he was letting Caz get her hands on those blueprints. And from the look in her eyes, Caz was thinking the same thing.

'I'm in,' she said.

'Me too,' said Zac.

'Excellent,' said Voler, clasping his hands together. 'We begin in three hours.'

Zac glanced at his watch.

6.57 A.M.

Voler smiled again and picked up his knife and fork.

'Now then,' he said brightly, 'time to eat this breakfast! You've got a big day ahead of you and you're going to need all the energy you can get.'

CHAPTER

'Here are the rules,' said Voler, pacing up and down in front of Zac and Caz.

They had finished breakfast, and now Voler's jet was hovering just above the Murky Swamp. Zac, Caz and Voler were down in the room full of flying machines, where Zac had first arrived.

'Rule number one,' said Voler. 'You may

go anywhere in the swamp and the forest.'

Zac nodded.

'Rule number two,' Voler continued. 'You are only allowed to take the equipment you were carrying when you arrived.'

Caz held up her Electromagnetic Whip and grinned nastily at Zac.

Zac felt around in his pocket for the SpyPad. *Lucky for me this thing is about a hundred gadgets in one,* he thought.

'Rule number three,' said Voler. 'You have until 6 p.m. to find the blueprints.'

Zac looked at the time.

9.59 A.M.

'What happens if neither of us has found the blueprints by then?' Zac asked.

'Then I will leave the pair of you behind and be on my way,' said Voler. 'And believe me when I say that you do *not* want to be stranded in the Murky Swamp after dark.'

Voler reached into his suit pocket. He pulled out two yellow envelopes and handed one each to Zac and Caz.

'Open these when you get down to the swamp,' Voler instructed. 'The clues inside will help you find the blueprints. I have also scattered a few other vehicles and so on around the swamp for you to uncover. You are allowed to use whatever you find.'

Voler pulled two green parachutes – or things that looked like parachutes – down from hooks on the wall. Each one was made from a big sheet of flexible plastic, stretched over a metal frame. The frames arched up in the middle, pulling the plastic into a dome shape.

'Put these on,' said Voler..

Zac took his parachute and strapped himself into the harness. Caz did the same.

'Excellent,' said Voler. 'Well, good luck!' He reached over and pulled a lever on the wall.

'Wait!' said Zac. 'What if –?'

HISSSS-**CLUNK!**

But then the metal trapdoor clanked open under Zac's feet and he was falling through the air. He reached up and firmly gripped the parachute cables.

FWOOMP!

The parachute filled up with air, slowing his fall.

Twisting his body left and right, Zac found that he could steer the parachute in any direction. He began gliding down towards the swamp in wide, lazy circles.

The flexible metal harness responded to his tiniest movements. It was almost like the parachute was part of his body.

This is incredible! thought Zac. *Why hasn't Leon come up with a design like this?*

There was a sudden flash of movement in front of Zac. Caz was speeding towards him on a collision course. She was trying to knock him out of the sky!

WHOOSH!

At the last second, Zac swooped clear of Caz's path. Caz went spinning through the air, only just managing to keep control of her parachute.

Trust Caz to play dirty, Zac thought to himself. He tilted his body forward, increasing his speed. He dived down towards the swamp, then pulled up at the last second and...

SPLASH!

He hit the muddy water feet-first and quickly began pulling off his parachute harness.

Moments later, Zac saw Caz splash down a few metres away.

Standing waist-deep in the water, Zac took Voler's envelope out of his pocket. He tore it open and pulled out three soggy cards with shapes printed on them.

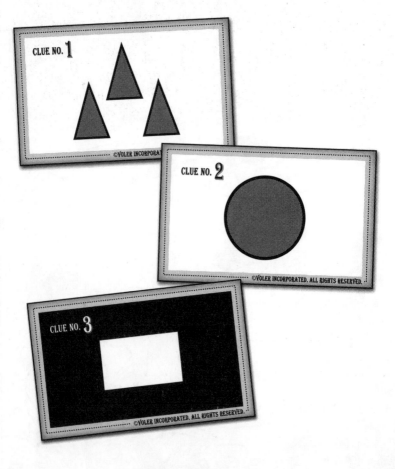

Great, thought Zac. *What on earth are these?*

He looked around at the swamp he had landed in. Dirty brown water stretched out in all directions. Here and there, little islands of mud rose up from the water.

Up ahead, way off in the distance, Zac could see a forest. And to his left, two enormous mountains stretched towards the sky.

Mountains! thought Zac, staring down at the first card. *Is that what these triangles are supposed to be?*

Caz seemed to think so. Looking around, Zac saw her splashing through the water in the direction of the mountains.

'I'll wait for you at the finish line, Agent Rock Star!' she called over her shoulder.

Zac was about to follow her when he noticed something. *Hold on*, he thought. *Why are there three triangles on the card and only TWO mountains?*

He peered around the swamp again. Maybe that wasn't the answer after all.

Then the forest in the distance caught Zac's eye again. What if those triangles on the card were meant to be trees?

Zac decided to follow his hunch.

He turned away from Caz and sprinted off in the direction of the forest.

CHAPTER 6

Hours later, Zac was still wading through the swamp in the direction of the trees.

He was almost there, but it was hard going. The hot sun beat down on him. There were spiky reeds growing everywhere. The mud at the bottom of the swamp grabbed at his feet with every step.

Zac was starting to wonder whether

he'd made the right choice after all.

SPLASH!

Zac whirled around, but there was nothing there. Just ripples on the water.

He was sure he'd heard something moving behind him. *Probably just a tree branch falling into the swamp,* he told himself. *Just concentrate on finding the blueprints.*

But then Zac felt something slither past his leg. Something big.

OK, he thought, *I definitely didn't imagine that.*

Zac started moving more quickly through the water, trying to get away from whatever was swimming around down there.

SPLASH!

'Aaahh!'

Something long and grey leapt up into the air in front of Zac, then splashed back down into the water.

An eel! Zac realised with a shudder.

But this was no ordinary eel. It was as thick as a tree trunk, with big pointed teeth. How was that even possible?

There must be something in the water, Zac thought. *Something toxic that makes the animals get like that.*

But he decided to leave the scientific explanations to Leon and concentrate on not getting eaten.

Up ahead, there was a huge fallen tree

poking out of the water. Zac waded over and pulled himself up on top of it.

Looking down, he saw the eel circling the tree, getting ready to leap up and attack again. *Eels are so gross,* he thought to himself, getting out his SpyPad.

He set it to Laser and pointed the SpyPad down at the water. Then he adjusted the beam setting to Maximum Power.

At first, the eel didn't seem to react. It just kept on swimming in circles around Zac. But then the water started to steam and bubble, boiling in the heat of the laser.

The eel leapt out of the water again. It let out an ear-splitting screech and snapped its jaws at Zac.

Zac ducked out of the way just in time, grabbing hold of a branch to steady himself.

SPLASH!

The horrible creature crashed down into the swamp and slithered away.

Zac let out a long sigh and waited for the water around him to cool down again. He scanned the area with his SpyPad.

No sign of Caz or the DSD.

Then Zac noticed something that made his eyes light up. It was one of the little mud islands that dotted the swamp. Most of these islands had only a few little bushes or weeds growing on them.

But this one was different. There were three trees sitting on top of it.

Zac pulled Voler's cards out of his pocket and glanced at the picture of the three triangles.

This must be it!

Zac dived down into the water and hurried across to the mud island. He climbed up between the trees and looked around for some clue about what to do next.

'If these trees are the triangles,' Zac said, thinking out loud, 'then the next thing I need to find is something round.'

PEOOWW!

Great, thought Zac. *Now what?*

His eyes flashed to the sky. Hovering through the air towards him was what looked like a black metal soccer ball.

Well, I guess that would be the round thing I'm supposed to be looking for.

Unfortunately, this particular round thing also happened to be firing lasers straight at him.

Zac crouched down behind one of the trees.

Zac had seen Voler use a weapon a bit like this before, the first time they had met. He knew that it had motion sensors which triggered the laser blasts. It was called a Laser Orb.

PEOOWW!

Another blast from the Laser Orb shattered the tree into splinters.

Don't move, Zac reminded himself. *If I don't move, it can't see me.*

Zac froze on the spot, his fingers digging into a pile of sticky mud on the ground. The Laser Orb hovered closer to him.

It spun around slowly, looking for any sign of movement.

Closer, closer…

Suddenly, Zac leapt up into the air and threw a massive glob of mud at the Orb's motion sensors.

SPLAT!

The Orb shuddered in mid-air, then hovered quietly on the spot.

Zac stood up slowly, making sure the motion sensors really were disabled.

But the mud had stuck and was now drying over the Orb.

'Congratulations, Zachary,' said a familiar voice. It was Voler. His voice was coming from a speaker inside the Orb.

CLUNK! CLUNK!

Two small handles had suddenly appeared from underneath the Orb.

'Well?' said Voler's voice. 'What are you waiting for?'

Zac stared at the Orb floating above his head. Then he leapt into the air, grabbing hold of the handles.

Shuddering slightly under Zac's weight, the Orb lifted him into the air and zoomed away across the swamp.

CHAPTER 7

For the second time that day, Zac found himself soaring high above the Murky Swamp. Voler's Laser Orb was surprisingly fast, and not easy to hold onto. Zac's arms quickly got tired, and a couple of times he almost lost his grip.

The Orb zoomed through the air, guiding Zac past more and more of the same endless swamp. But there was still no sign of the plastic toad with the DSD inside.

This place is massive, thought Zac. *Those blueprints could be anywhere!*

VROOOOOM!

Zac looked back over his shoulder. Caz was beneath him, sitting aboard a shiny orange hovercraft!

That must be one of the vehicles that Voler left for us to find, Zac realised.

The hovercraft tore across the swamp, bucking and bouncing, sending an enormous spray of water out behind it.

Caz looked up and saw Zac hovering above her. She shot him a look of pure hatred. But she seemed to decide that Zac was heading in the right direction. Caz brought the hovercraft around, ready to chase after Zac.

But Zac was moving too quickly for her. The Laser Orb kept on pulling him through the air, and before long Caz was just a speck in the distance.

Still clinging to the Orb, Zac craned his neck to look up at his watch.

In just over three hours, Voler's jet would fly away and Zac would be stranded in the swamp. And who knew where this flying ball was taking him? Zac began to wonder whether he should just let go of the Orb and continue his search back on the ground.

But the Orb had other ideas.

WHOOOOOSH!

Suddenly, the Laser Orb took a sharp turn to the right. Zac's left hand slipped off the Orb and he had to scramble to get his grip back.

Now Zac could see the end of the swamp coming into view below him. Tall trees grew up from the mud like a green wall, all along the water's edge. With a jolt, Zac felt the Orb begin flying downwards. It was coming in to land.

Zac flew lower and lower, until his feet were almost touching the surface of the water. The Orb reached the swamp's edge and came to a stop between two trees.

I guess I'm here, thought Zac, dropping to the ground. *Wherever 'here' is.*

As soon as Zac let go of the Orb, it whizzed up into the sky and flew away.

Zac pulled out Voler's clues again. The last card was all dark except for a white rectangle. He started walking through the trees, looking for anything that might be a good match.

Walking deeper into the forest, Zac saw a shape that looked darker than the trees around it. He walked over for a closer look. It was the entrance to a big stony cave. Zac's spy senses tingled.

He switched on his SpyPad's torch and stepped inside.

Zac's torch wasn't the only light in the cave. Further inside the cave, something else was glowing.

Zac headed in the direction of the light. *Is there someone else in here?* he wondered. Surely there was no way Caz could have overtaken him!

Zac rounded a corner and finally found the source of the light. It was an enormous computer screen showing a map of the Murky Swamp.

Ah, Zac thought to himself. *The screen must be the white square on the clue card.*

The map on the screen was black and white – except for one little island that was glowing bright red.

That must be where the X-Beam blueprints are hidden! Zac realised. He quickly pulled out his SpyPad and carefully snapped a photo of the map. But then a sudden noise from outside broke his concentration.

Back out in the swamp, someone had just let out a terrified, ear-splitting scream.

CHAPTER

Zac raced out of the cave and back towards the swamp. He reached the edge of the water and saw right away who had been screaming.

It was Caz. She was standing aboard her little hovercraft, cracking her Electro-magnetic Whip at a massive crocodile.

Caz brought the whip down again

and again, sending sparks flying. But the crocodile didn't even seem to notice that it was being hit.

The hovercraft rocked back and forth, and Zac could see that it was only a matter of time before the croc knocked Caz right into the water.

Zac sighed. He knew what he had to do.

He jumped back into the swamp and began wading out. *Towards* the crocodile.

But as he got closer, he realised that it wasn't a real crocodile at all. Instead of scales, the croc was covered in grey steel plating. Instead of eyes, two red lights blinked menacingly in Caz's direction.

It was a robotic crocodile! It must have

been planted there by Professor Voler.

As if the real animals in this place aren't bad enough! thought Zac, remembering the eel.

He crept up behind the robocodile, trying to keep from being seen. Zac remembered something he'd seen on Leon's favourite nature show, *Creepy Creatures*.

Zac leapt up onto the robocodile's back, just as it took another lunge at Caz.
CLANK!

The robocodile's mouth snapped shut. Zac grabbed onto the closed jaws and held on tight.

For a second he thought his plan had

worked. But then the robocodile snapped its mouth open again, flipped Zac over and threw him into the swamp.

SPLASH!

I guess that rule only works for real crocodiles, thought Zac, getting to his feet. He decided to switch on his Electro-Armour just to be safe.

Caz cowered on the hovercraft, but the robocodile had already started swimming towards Zac.

Zac turned and ran through the shallow water, but his feet kept slipping into the mud, slowing him down. In seconds, the robocodile was right on top of him. It stretched its mouth wide. Looking up,

Zac saw row after row of razor-sharp steel teeth.

Uh-oh, he thought, trying to dart out of the way. But the robocodile lunged right for him. Its mechanical jaws came down on top of Zac, right across his chest.

CLANK!

Luckily, Zac's arms were up in the air, and the robocodile's metal teeth crunched down hard on his Electro-Armour.

KZZZZZK-POW!

The armour sent a surge of electricity into the robocodile's mouth. The croc shot up into the air, twisting and sparking. Zac could see that its systems had been fried instantly.

SPLASH!

Zac dived out of the way as the roboc-odile came crashing into the water, completely destroyed.

Zac stood up and paddled over to Caz's hovercraft.

'I thought you were done for,' said Caz, sounding almost disappointed that the croc hadn't finished him off. 'He bit you straight across the chest! How'd you survive that?'

Zac lifted up his shirt to reveal the Electro-Armour hiding underneath.

'Hey!' Caz protested. 'How come you've got *armour?*'

'I wouldn't be complaining if I were

you,' said Zac. 'This armour just saved your life!'

'Well, I'm fine now,' said Caz, crossing her arms. 'So you can get out of here.'

But when Zac looked down and saw the time, he knew it wasn't going to be that simple.

4.01 P.M.

There were only two hours left! He cringed as he realised what he was going to have to do next.

'Well?' said Caz. 'What are you waiting for? Get lost!'

'No,' said Zac. 'Let me onto that hovercraft.'

'Yeah, right,' Caz laughed.

'I know where the plastic toad is hidden,' said Zac. 'But we're going to have to go together.'

'I'm not going anywhere with you, Rock Star,' Caz growled.

'You think *I* want to be stuck with *you*?' said Zac. 'In two hours, Voler's going to fly off and leave us both behind. You can't even stay alive in the *daytime* without my help. Do you really want to be stuck here at night?'

'No-one *asked* you to help me,' Caz spat. 'I had it all under control.'

'Really?' said Zac, raising an eyebrow.

Caz glared at Zac, but was silent.

'Look,' Zac said, trying to keep calm.

'You've got the hovercraft, but no idea where the plastic toad is. I've got a map to the plastic toad but no way to get there. The only way we can get out of here is if we work together.'

Caz stared at him, weighing up her options. Then she let out a groan of disgust.

'Fine,' she said. 'Get on.'

CHAPTER 9

The hovercraft tore across the surface of the swamp, towards the island where the X-Beam blueprints were hidden.

VROOOOOM!

Even though it was Zac who knew the way to the island, Caz had refused to let him drive. So Zac sat looking over Caz's shoulder, shouting directions over the roar of the engine. He kept his SpyPad hidden in his pocket, and only checked the map when he was sure Caz wasn't looking.

Apart from that, they kept silent.

They may have been working together now, but they both knew that their agreement would be over as soon as they stepped off the hovercraft.

Even now, sitting behind Caz, Zac was half-tempted to shove her overboard and drive off without her. But he sighed instead and checked the time.

5.32 P.M.

'Right!' he shouted to Caz. 'No, wait – turn left!'

Everything looked so different from the

ground. It was hard to figure out which way they were supposed to be going.

But then he saw it. Up ahead was an island of mud with two big trees knocked down and arranged into the shape of an X.

X marks the spot, thought Zac. This had to be it.

'Over there!' he called.

Caz guided the hovercraft over to the island and brought it to a stop.

Zac stood up and reached for his SpyPad, ready to check the map one last time.

CRACK!

Caz lashed Zac across the back with her whip. Zac's Electro-Armour sparked and kept him from getting hurt, but the impact was enough to send him staggering overboard.

SPLASH!

Zac got to his feet and clambered up onto the island, right behind Caz.

Caz raced around the island, searching frantically for Voler's plastic toad.

Zac, meanwhile, headed straight for the centre of the X-shape made by the fallen trees. He found a patch of long, brown grass and started digging through it.

His hand caught on something that was sticking up out of the ground. Brushing the grass aside, Zac saw that it was a rusty metal lever. He took a deep breath and pulled.

THUD!

Caz ran over and shoved Zac aside, knocking him to the ground. She grabbed the lever for herself and started heaving at it with all her might.

Zac scrambled to his feet and tried to pry Caz's hands off the handle.

'Get off, Rock Star!' growled Caz. 'Those blueprints are *mine*.'

Both of them were holding onto the handle now, trying to shove each other away and pull on the lever at the same time.

Slowly the lever started to shift. CREEEAAK!

They dragged it up and over, until it was pointing away in the opposite direction.

For a moment, nothing happened.

Zac and Caz let go of the lever and stepped apart from each other.

Then, a few metres away, the swamp started to bubble and churn. A strange clattering sound came up from under the water. Then something big and round started rising slowly up out of the swamp.

At first, the thing was so covered in mud that they couldn't see what it was. But then the mud started dripping back down into the swamp, revealing a big glass dome.

Inside the dome, sitting on top of a stone platform, was a neatly folded Chopper Suit. It was just like the one that Zac had used to board Voler's jet that morning.

Walking to the edge of the island for

a closer look, Zac noticed something else sitting on the platform.

It was a small plastic toad. The blueprints must be hidden inside!

Zac glanced at Caz. She had seen it, too.

But before either of them could react, they were distracted by another sound.

WHOOMF-WHOOMF!

Someone was coming down out of the sky towards them, wearing a Chopper Suit. It was Professor Voler.

Voler touched down on the island and looked from Zac to Caz.

'Well, well,' he said with a grin. 'A GIB agent and a BIG agent working together! I never thought I'd see the day.'

CHAPTER 10

'Working together?' Caz laughed. 'I was only using him to get to the blueprints!'

Zac's eyes were fixed on Voler. The professor tapped at the controls on his sleeve, and the helicopter blades folded back into his Chopper Suit.

'Please don't let me interrupt,' said Voler, grinning at the two of them. 'I just thought I'd come down here for a closer view of the big finish.'

CREEEAAK!

Zac's eyes flashed across to the dome in the swamp. The glass was splitting apart. He leapt into the water and splashed towards the dome, with Caz right behind him.

Zac and Caz reached the dome at the same time and dived for the plastic toad. They crashed down onto the platform, hands grabbing wildly.

Zac felt his fingers close around the toad. *Yes!*

SPLASH!

Caz barrelled into Zac and they tumbled into the water. Zac wriggled free of her and made his way back up onto the island.

He slipped the plastic toad into his pocket, right next to his SpyPad. Looking back over his shoulder, he saw Caz climbing up out of the water.

Then Zac realised his mistake. He may have got his hands on the plastic toad, but Caz had taken the spare Chopper Suit.

'Well now, this *is* an interesting twist!' said Voler, smiling at Zac. 'You've tracked down my X-Beam blueprints, but now you've got no way of escaping the swamp.'

Voler turned to Caz.

'And *you've* got the Chopper Suit, but no blueprints,' he said. 'How do you suppose you're going to –?'

CRACK!

In a flash, Caz had switched on her Electromagnetic Whip and cracked it at Voler. The cord of electricity struck the big round 'REMOVE' button on the chest of his Chopper Suit.

SNAP!

The Chopper Suit popped right off Voler and landed in a crumpled heap in the grass. Caz reached down and grabbed the suit before Voler had time to react.

'Wait!' said Voler, looking furious. 'You can't do that! It's not in the rules!'

'It is now,' sneered Caz.

Voler shot Caz a dangerous look. But Caz waved her whip at him and he backed off. Then she walked across to Zac, carrying the two Chopper Suits.

'Here's the deal,' she said. 'You hand over the toad and I give you one of these suits.'

Zac looked across at Voler, who was staring angrily at them. Zac had just remembered something and he was sure Caz wouldn't like it!

Fighting the urge to grin, he looked back at Caz and sighed loudly.

'I guess giving up the plastic toad is the only way I'm going to get out of here,' he said, shrugging. 'OK, it's a deal.'

He pulled the toad from his pocket and handed it to Caz. Then he grabbed one of her Chopper Suits and put it on.

'I hope you two have learnt a lesson today,' said Caz, slipping into her own Chopper Suit and backing away from them. *'Don't mess with BIG!'*

She tapped at the suit's controls and started rising up into the air. Zac took one last look at Voler and followed her.

'See you later, Agent Rock Star!' called Caz over her shoulder. 'Better luck next time!'

But Zac just grinned at her and waved.

Caz stopped mid-air. 'What are you smiling at?' she demanded.

'Nothing,' said Zac. 'I'm just thinking of all the awesome stuff I'm going to do with my new X-Beam.'

'What are you talking about?' Caz glared, holding up the plastic toad. 'I've got the blueprints right here!'

'Yeah, about that,' said Zac. 'When I put the plastic toad in my pocket, my SpyPad wirelessly transmitted the blueprints to GIB HQ! It's an automatic function.'

Caz stared at him, mouth open.

'And then it wiped all the data from the DSD,' added Zac. 'But don't worry, I'm sure your boss will find all kinds of useful things to do with a plastic toad!'

Zac spun his Chopper Suit around and flew away, laughing. Caz let out an angry shout and disappeared in the opposite direction.

Still chuckling to himself, Zac looked back towards the swamp. He saw Voler's jet shimmer into view above the island. His bodyguard must have been coming to rescue him.

I don't think Voler's game turned out quite according to plan, Zac thought. Then he felt his SpyPad vibrate in his pocket.

Excellent, he smirked to himself. *That's probably HQ calling to congratulate me.*

He pulled out the SpyPad. It was Agent Blizzard, the babysitter.

'Well done, Zac!' she said brightly. 'Now come straight home, please!'

'Thanks,' said Zac. 'Wait – what? Where are Mum and Dad?'

Agent Blizzard grinned in the screen of Zac's SpyPad. 'Your parents thought I did such a good job babysitting that they've decided to leave me in charge *again* tonight!'

Zac sighed. As if he needed a babysitter! *Well,* he thought, *at least flying home in my new Chopper Suit will be fun.*

'Oh, and I almost forgot,' said Agent Blizzard. 'You didn't finish your chores last night. When you get back, you've got some washing to fold!'